SECURITY

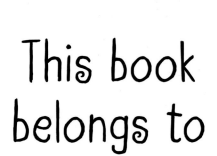

This book belongs to

_____

The Wilderness, Berkhamsted, Hertfordshire, HP4 2AZ, UK.
501 Nelson Place, P.O. Box 141000, Nashville, TN 37214-1000, USA.

Written by Rosie Greening.
Illustrated by Stuart Lynch.

NEVER touch A T. rex

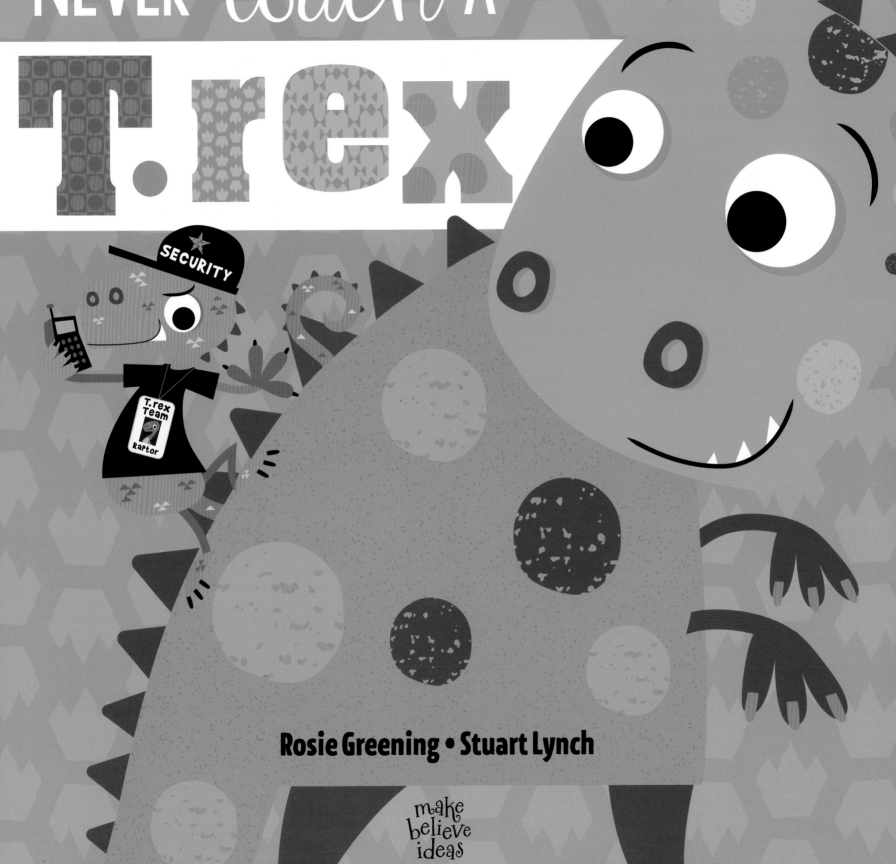

SECURITY

T. rex Team Raptor

Rosie Greening • Stuart Lynch

make believe ideas

WELL YOU CAN'T.

Here's the rule:

① You must never touch a T. rex, unless you . . .

. . . point to your nose.

There's no way you can point to your nose. Just you try!

How did you do that?

Okay, this is the **real** rule.
You must **never** touch a **T. rex**,
unless you . . .

. . . POINT to your nose

and TOUCH your toes!

Ha! Try those if you
think you're so clever.

Okay, genius.

The actual rule is this:

Never touch a T. rex,

unless you . . .

SECURITY

T. rex Team

Raptor

...point to your nose,

touch your toes,

and find a rose.

GOTCHA!

You won't find a **rose** on this page.

Right. **EVEN YOU won't be able to . . .**

. . . point to your nose,

SECURITY

T.rex Team Raptor

touch your toes,

find a rose,

and shout,

"Banana!"

Have you done this before?

It's **lucky** I have a plan . . .

You must never touch a **T. rex,**
unless you . . .

find
a
rose,

**touch
your toes,**

I **COUNT** 2
to three, 3

Wave
at me,

. . . point
to your
nose,

Shout,
"BANANA!"

GLUE

meow
like a cat,
SECURITY
FLAP
like a
BAT,
T.rex
Team
Raptor
sing HIGH,
then low,
SAAAAAAY
SOOOMETHIIIIING
SLOOOOOWWWW . . .

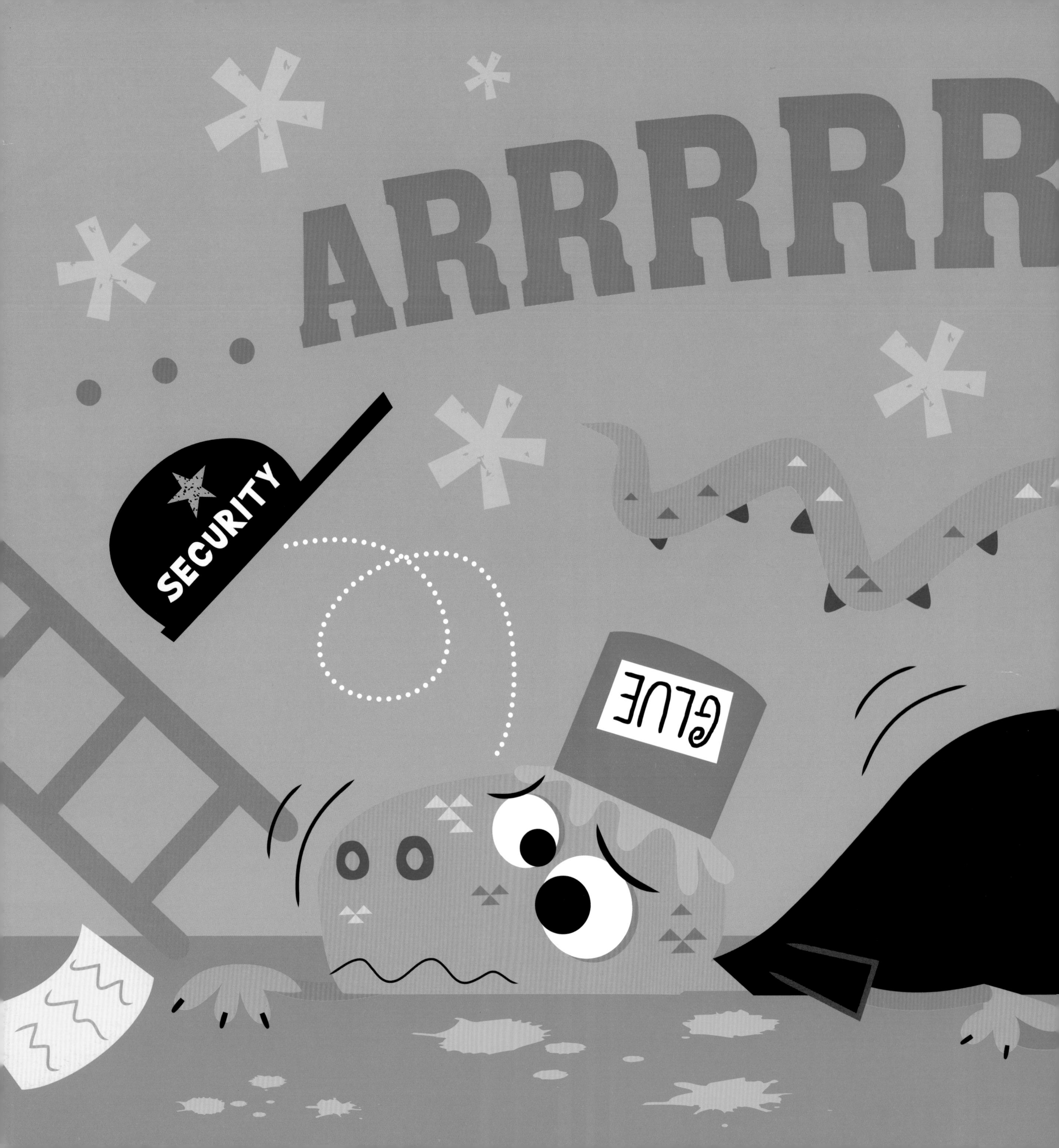

ARRRRR
SECURITY
GLUE

"**HELLO!**

Sorry about the guard.

There's really only **one** rule you need to know.

You must **never** touch a T. rex, unless you . . .

ASK POLITELY.

Go on, **give it a try!**"

"How **nice** and **polite** you are!

OF COURSE
YOU CAN!"

Okay, okay.

You're brighter than I thought.
But I've got one more rule for you:

DON'T CLOSE
this book!

THE END

SECURITY